CUENTO
DE LUZ

To Pau Conde,
who slays purple dragons.

- Carmen Gil -

For my little heroes: Joel, Edith, and Gabriel,
who have already slain mighty dragons.

- Marta Munté -

Text © Carmen Gil
Illustrations © Marta Munté
This edition © 2014 Cuento de Luz SL
Calle Claveles 10 | Urb Monteclaro | Pozuelo de Alarcón | 28223 | Madrid | Spain
www.cuentodeluz.com
Title in Spanish: Kibo y el dragón morado
English translation by Jon Brokenbrow

ISBN: 978-84-16078-24-0

Printed by Shanghai Chenxi Printing Co., Ltd. April 2014, print number 1426-2

FSC
www.fsc.org
MIX
Paper from
responsible sources
FSC® C007923

KIBO

AND

THE PURPLE DRAGON

CARMEN GIL

MARTA MUNTÉ

Kibo liked three things more than anything else in the world: feeding lettuce leaves to his tortoise, zooming down the slide in the park, and making funny faces in front of the mirror in his bedroom.

One morning, Kibo invented a new funny face—making his ears stick out and touching the tip of his nose with his tongue. As soon as he finished his breakfast, he ran upstairs and sat smiling to himself in front of the mirror.

But as he was stretching his tongue and pulling on his ears, something dreadful happened. A scaly, purple dragon climbed in through his open window. And in the twinkling of an eye, it reared up behind Kibo, like a shadow.

Kibo was so frightened he started to run.

He ran all the way to the huge tree
in the square, which everyone said
was home to an elf;

past the old abandoned house
that made strange, spooky noises;

and around the fountain
with the seven spouts
and the lemon-flavored water.

But when he returned home and looked at
himself in the mirror, the dragon was still
there, right behind him! It was a little
bigger and a little purpler than the last time.

"What am I going to do?" said Kibo. He thought and thought, until suddenly he had a great idea.

"I'll go all the way around the world. There's no way the purple dragon can follow me."

So he grabbed his backpack, put on his stripy T-shirt, and without daring to look back, ran out of his house, ready to see the world.

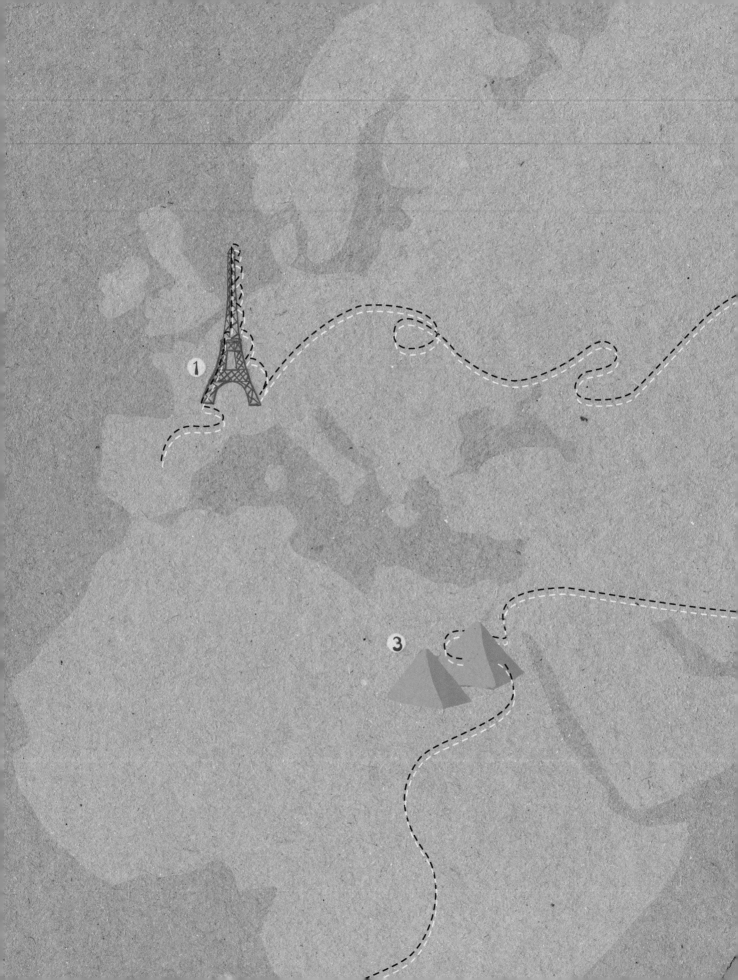

Kibo climbed more than sixteen hundred steps to the top of the Eiffel Tower, walked the entire length of the Great Wall of China, and entered the labyrinths of an Egyptian pyramid.

Then he walked across the whole African savannah, hiked for three days to reach Machu Picchu, and rode in the elevator to the top of the Empire State Building. Way up there, seeing how the spire on the top of the skyscraper was tickling the belly of a passing evening cloud, he decided it was time to go back home.

But when he got home and looked at himself in the mirror, the purple dragon was still there, right behind him. It was a little bigger and a little purpler than the last time he'd seen it.

"How am I going to get rid of this monster?" Kibo asked himself.
He thought and thought about it, until he found an answer.

"Of course. That's it! However purple it is, no dragon can follow me all the way to Mars!"

In his glittering silver space suit and spaceship, Kibo reached Mars, the red planet. He walked past craters, lava fields, and volcanoes.

He met a Martian with one eye and four feet,
who told awful jokes.

"How can you tell which end of a worm is which?
Tickle it in the middle, and see which end laughs!"

Traveling at the speed of light, Kibo continued on his interplanetary voyage. His ship nearly burned up when he passed Venus! With its thick layer of clouds, it was the hottest of all the planets. And the brightest! He had looked at it out of his bedroom window so many times. "It's the evening star," his mom would say. And Kibo would close his eyes as tightly as he could and make a wish.

"I want the dragon to disappear," was what he wished this time.

And at the speed of light, he returned home.

Back in his bedroom, Kibo walked toward his mirror with his head hanging down. As he raised his eyes, there was the dragon. A little bigger and a little purpler than the last time.

"What am I going to do now?" he asked himself.

He thought and thought until steam started to come out of his ears, and then suddenly yelled, "I've got it! I'll go to the bottom of the sea!"

Wearing his diver's suit, Kibo swam down until he reached a field of waving sea grass. There he saw snails, starfish, sea urchins, and crabs. He could hardly believe his eyes when he met Dugong, a huge merman with a round, friendly face, who invited him to a delicious seaweed banquet.

After eating roast seaweed, boiled seaweed, and fried seaweed, Kibo felt that it was time to go home.

Soaked to the skin, and standing in front of the mirror in his bedroom once again, he saw that the dragon was still behind him. A little bigger and a little purpler than the last time.

"Is there any way to get rid of him?" he asked himself.
After racking his brain for hours and hours, a huge
smile suddenly spread over his face.

"Of course! Why didn't I think of it before!
The best way to get rid of a monster
is to stop thinking about it!"

So Kibo picked up a book of fairy tales, the biggest one he could find on the shelf, and started reading it.

Suddenly he was immersed in a world of elves, magicians, Knights, and witches riding on broomsticks.

He met Maggie the fairy, who instead of turning frogs into princes, turned them into fried eggs.

And he met Princess Bonnie, who was completely fed up with her knight in shining armor.

But like every other book, this one had an ending. When he finished the book, Kibo once again felt the dragon's presence.

And when he looked in the mirror, there it was!

Bigger and purpler than ever.

Tired of trying to run away, Kibo decided it was time to face up to the dragon. He took a deep, deep breath, clenched his teeth together, went as red as a tomato, and turned his head around!

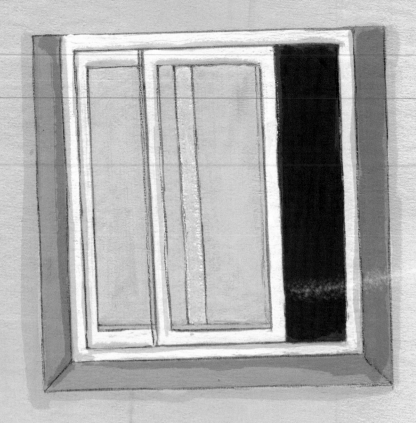

That was when the miracle happened. When Kibo looked into the dragon's eyes, face-to-face, it shot out of the window, dragging a huge suitcase behind it. He suddenly felt as light as a feather, and jumped with joy.

And do you know what they say? That inside of his suitcase, the dragon had all of Kibo's fears.

When you see a dragon,
One thing is quite clear,
If you look them in the eye
They'll run away in fear.

That evening, without any fear in his heart, Kibo could do the three things he liked best in the world: feed lettuce leaves to his tortoise, zoom headfirst down the slide, and make funny faces in front of the mirror in his bedroom.